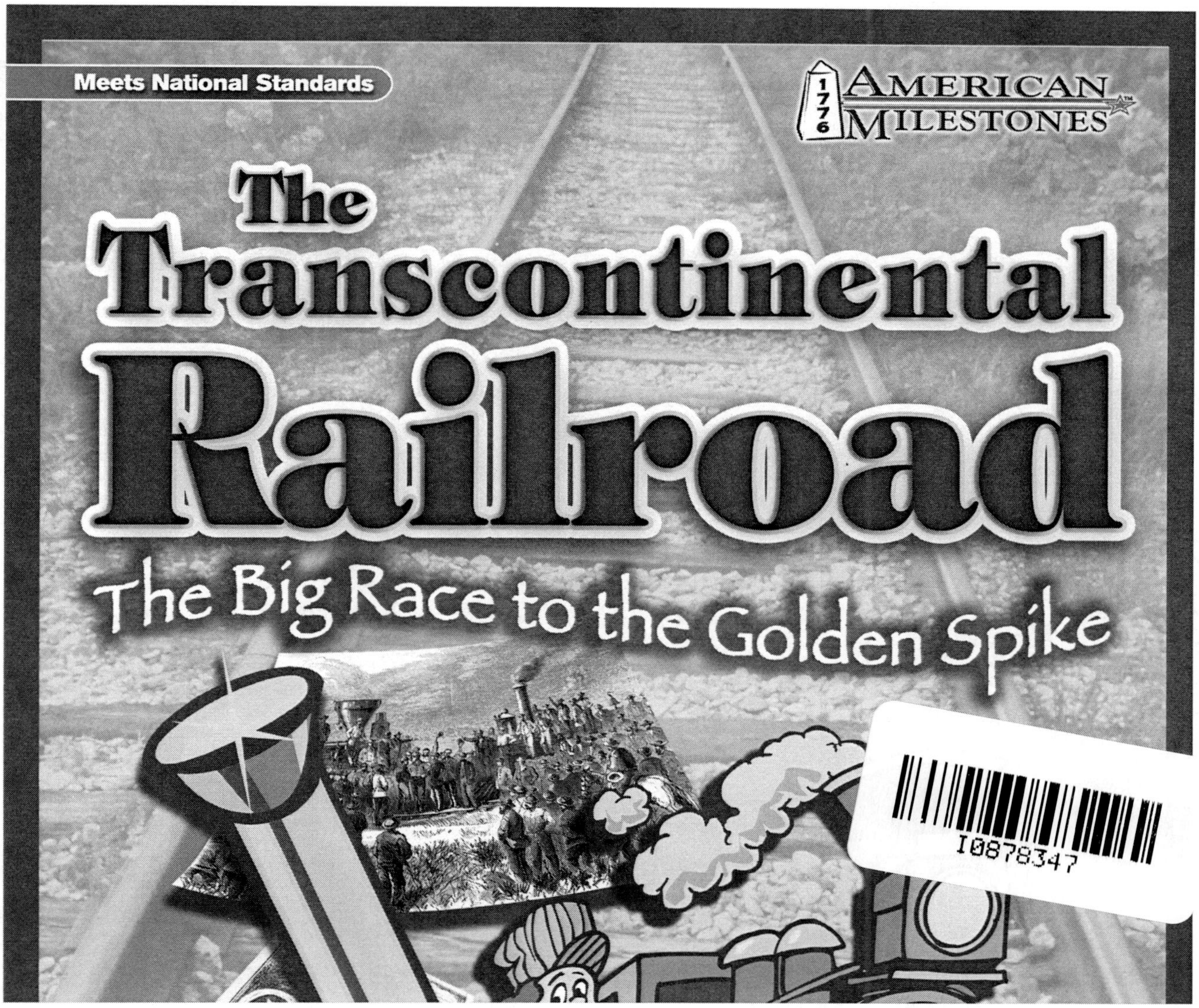

©2010 Paperback ISBN: 978-0-635-07506-2
©2010 Library Binding ISBN: 978-0-635-07550-5

Gallopade is proud to be a member of these educational organizations and associations:

American Library Association (ALA)
The National School Supply and Equipment Association (NSSEA)
The National Council for the Social Studies (NCSS)
National Association for Gifted Children (NAGC)
American Booksellers Association (ABA)
Museum Store Association (MSA)
International Reading Association (IRA)
Supporter of **Association of Partners for Public Lands (APPL)**

Published by
GALLOPADE™ INTERNATIONAL
800-536-2GET
www.gallopade.com

CAROLE MARSH BOOKS

Other Carole Marsh Books

Orville & Wilbur Wright . . . Step Out Into The Sky!
Lewis & Clark Go On a Hike: The Story of the Corps of Discovery
The Louisiana Purchase: "What A Deal!"
The American Revolution: How Our Nation Was Born
The American Civil War: When Brother Fought Brother
The U.S. Civil Rights Movement: The Fight For Equality
The Bill of Rights: "It Can't Be Wrong!"
U.S. Constitution: "Sign on the Dotted Line!"
The Declaration of Independence: "Quit Bossing Us Around!"
Jamestown: America's First Permanent English Settlement
The Underground Railroad: Path to Freedom
Industrial Revolution: From Muscles to Machines!
Great Depression & the New Deal: Brother, Can You Spare a Dime?
World War II: When Men, Women, and Children Saved the World
Brown v. Board of Education: I Want to Go to School!
World War I: The War to End All Wars!
Abraham Lincoln: America's 16th President
The U.S. Supreme Court: The Keepers of the Laws of Our Land
Galloping West with the Pony Express!: "The Mail Must Go Through!"
The Transcontinental Railroad: The Big Race to the Golden Spike!
The 13 Colonies: A New Life in a New World!
Wagons Ho! Pioneers' Path to the West!: The Oregon Trail

State Stuff™, Available for all 50 states:

My First Pocket Guide
State My First Book
State Wheel of Fortune Gamebook
State Survivor Gamebook
State Illustrated Timelines
"Jography!": A Fun Run Through Our State
The State Coloring Book
The Big Reproducible Activity Book
State Millionaire Gamebook
State Project Books
Jeopardy: Answers & Questions About Our State

Patriotic Favorites™

Patriotic Favorites Coloring Book
Patriotic Biographies
The Daily Patriot: 365 Quotations
Young Patriots Coloring & Activity Book
Patriotic Projects
Patriotisms: 365 Definitions

Table of Contents

A Word from the Author

Dear Reader,

I've always wanted to ride a train! No, not the Choo-Choo Express at a kiddie amusement park, or a heart-stopping roller coaster-type ride. I just want to ride a regular passenger train. And I want to ride it across the country. Why? Because I want to look out the window as we fly by meadows, forests, towns, and rivers. And if we have to climb over a mountain, I won't close my eyes, even though I'm not a big fan of heights! I think seeing things from a train car would give me a whole different perspective on our country; one that I couldn't get peering down on it from high in the sky or staring out the window of a cramped car.

The masterminds behind the Transcontinental Railroad had more urgent needs in mind when they decided it was time for a railroad that connected our country. The United States was growing quickly. People desperately needed a better way to get from coast to coast than a seven-month trip by covered wagon. It seemed like an impossible task! Those tracks had to cover nearly 2,000 miles and cross a mountain range. Along the way there were angry Native Americans, dangerous weather, and wild animals! But as so many Americans before them had done, the men and women behind the Transcontinental Railroad persevered, and taught us many important things:

- Dream big!
- Have a plan!
- Keep going!

These courageous Americans weren't the first to accomplish something extraordinary. And of course they won't be the last! Ride along with me, and learn about one of the most amazing success stories in American history!

All Aboard!

Carole Marsh

A Timeline of Events

1841 Settlers start moving west across the northern Great Plains. The route they take will become known as the Oregon Trail.

December 1848 President James K. Polk announces the discovery of gold in the Oregon Territory. The race is on for expansion to the West!

July 1860 Engineer Theodore Judah reaches Donner Pass. He realizes it is the perfect location for building a railway through the Sierra Nevada mountain range.

November 1860 Judah convinces businessman Collis P. Huntington, from Sacramento, California, to join in his railroad project. Four other men (Mark Hopkins, James Bailey, Charles Crocker, and Leland Stanford) also join the team. This is the first board of directors of the Central Pacific Railroad company.

1862 President Abraham Lincoln signs the Pacific Railroad Act. This act authorizes the construction of the first transcontinental railroad.

January 8, 1863 Leland Stanford, now the governor of California, shovels the first load of dirt at the Central Pacific groundbreaking ceremony in Sacramento.

December 2, 1863 The Union Pacific Railroad breaks ground in Omaha, Nebraska. It doesn't actually go anywhere for several more years!

1865 Chinese immigrants begin working on the Central Pacific Railroad. By the time the project is finished they are considered the heroes of this western segment of the Transcontinental Railroad!

May 10, 1869 The Central Pacific and Union Pacific railroads come together at Promontory Summit, Utah. Leland Stanford drives a golden spike into the ground so that everyone will remember the amazing event!

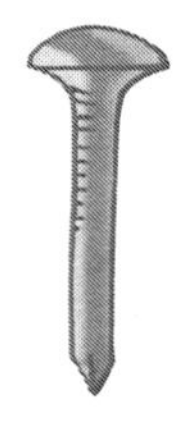

The Transcontinental Railroad:
The Big Race to the Golden Spike!

DING DONG! Andrew Barr listened with excitement to the ringing bells. Those bells announced the amazing news to his hometown of Sacramento, California. Today, May 10, 1869, work on the Transcontinental Railroad was finally complete! The tracks that met in Promontory, Utah joined the East and the West!

Andrew knew how important this moment was! His family had journeyed from Kentucky to California just a few years earlier. The trip by covered wagon had taken nearly seven months, and was full of danger! It was so dangerous that his grandmother had stayed behind.

Andrew had heard that the new railroad meant the trip across the country could now be made in less than a week–and from the comfort and safety of a train car!

Maybe Grandmother could finally join them!

Railroad Facts

A railroad is a system of transportation. It is made up of trains, tracks, stations, and other equipment. Railroads can carry large cargo over long distances in a single trip.

The history of the railroad goes way back! The ancient Greeks used deep grooves in the ground to move heavy wagons. Early Europeans used handcarts on wooden rails to transport things.

The first modern railroads were built nearly 40 years before the Transcontinental Railroad joined the East and the West in the United States! The Tom Thumb was the first steam locomotive in the United States. It began carrying passengers and goods the 13-mile distance between Baltimore, Maryland, and Ellicott's Mills, Maryland, in 1830!

From Here to There!

Railroads are a method of transportation, or a way to get from one place to another. List all the methods of transportation you can think of. (Hint: Not all methods of transportation are mechanical!)

FAST FACT: A train is a group of connected railroad cars that are powered by steam, diesel fuel, or electricity. A locomotive is normally the engine car out front. A caboose is the car that is usually last!

Follow the Oregon Trail!

Before the Transcontinental Railroad, pioneers traveling from the eastern United States to the western territories followed a path called the Oregon Trail. The 2,000-mile dirt path began in Missouri and ended in Oregon City. Along the way, it wound through prairies and crossed roaring rivers. It even passed up and over mountain ranges!

The pioneers bumped along the Oregon Trail for months in covered wagons pulled by oxen. They took food that would not spoil along the way. Beans, rice, dried meat, dried fruit, and hardtack (hard, dried bread which had to be softened in water to eat) were popular choices. Most of their cooking was done over open campfires using buffalo chips for fuel. These "chips" were really dried buffalo poop!

Most children didn't have time for school while they were traveling the Oregon Trail! How would you like that?!

Meals to Go!

Pioneers liked beef jerky because it was tasty. And because it was made with lots of salt, it didn't spoil easily. Try this beef jerky recipe at home. Remember to have an adult help you!

Ingredients:
1 flank steak or London broil steak
salt and pepper
1 cup soy sauce
aluminum foil

Directions:
Set your oven to 150 degrees. Cut the steak into strips with the grain of the meat. If you don't cut along the grain, the cooked meat will fall apart into tiny pieces! Pour the soy sauce into a bowl and dip the meat strips in it. Lay the strips out on a piece of foil and sprinkle them generously with salt and pepper on both sides. Place the strips on a metal rack in the oven with foil below to catch the drippings. Bake for 10 hours. Enjoy!

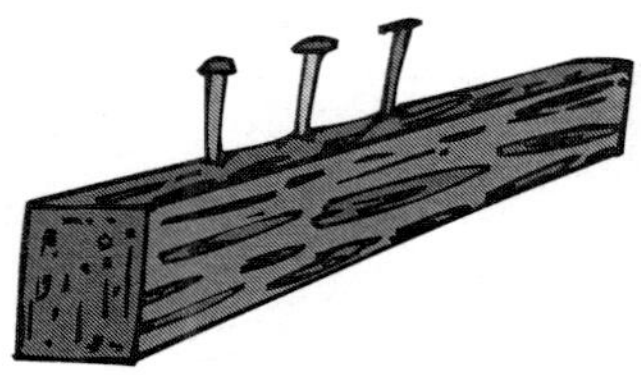

Why a Transcontinental Railroad?

One of the greatest adventures in American history began on July 1, 1862, when President Abraham Lincoln signed the Pacific Railroad Act! This important law gave permission to start building a railroad that connected the country!

People had known for many years that it was important to find a way to travel quickly from the East Coast to the western United States. When gold was discovered in California in 1849, people began flocking to the West to get rich! A cross-country railroad was really important now!

The plan was for the Union Pacific Railroad to build west from Omaha, Nebraska, and for the Central Pacific Railroad to come east from Sacramento, California. What no one could agree on was where the two lines should meet!

From 1866 to 1869, the two companies struggled to overcome rugged terrain, desert heat, freezing winters, and Indian attacks. Finally, leaders decided that the two lines would meet in Promontory, Utah. On May 10, 1869, a golden spike was driven into the ground where the two railroads met. The United States was connected at last!

Timeline!

Put these important events in the history of the Transcontinental Railroad in order!

___ Work begins on the Transcontinental Railroad

___ The Union Pacific and the Central Pacific Railroads meet in Promontory, Utah

___ Gold is discovered in California

___ President Lincoln signs the Pacific Railroad Act

___ People begin heading west to search for gold

___ Railroad workers battle Indians and dangerous weather

It's a Gold Rush!

When James Marshall found gold in the American River in 1848, he had no idea that people would soon be coming from everywhere to find their fortune in the Oregon Territory! That territory included the land that would soon become the state of California. It was the beginning of the California Gold Rush!

The people who came to search for gold were called prospectors. The people who stayed to dig for gold were called miners. Later, they were called Forty Niners. The location of Marshall's discovery grew with the Gold Rush, and became California's capital city of Sacramento.

Sacramento also became the starting point of the Central Pacific Railroad. The Central Pacific would join with the Union Pacific to connect the country!

Going for Gold!

Follow the directions below to learn how "panning for gold" was done.

Finding gold during the California Gold Rush was no easy job! Gold miners used a pan to scoop up soil and water from the river. Then they swirled away the dirt and sand. They were looking for tiny pieces of gold. This way of finding gold is called "panning." Gold miners panned a river to find out if they should mine in the area.

Try panning yourself! Gather small objects like paperclips, shells, tiny toys, erasers, and stones. Ask an adult for a small gold item like an earring. Put all the objects into a large, shallow dish. Add water and sand. Swish the objects around. What happens? Are the heaviest objects on the top or the bottom?

It Took a Team

It took thousands of people to build the Transcontinental Railroad! But the project started with the vision and determination of four men. Leland Stanford, Collis P. Huntington, Charles Crocker, and Mark Hopkins worked together to plan the railroad and to make sure the difficult and dangerous project was finished.

Each man had an important job to do! Huntington was in charge of asking Congress for the money to build the railroad. Crocker found a way to construct rails over giant mountains and across the burning deserts. Stanford kept track of all the details, and Hopkins made sure that none of the money was wasted.

Today, those men are known as "The Big Four"!

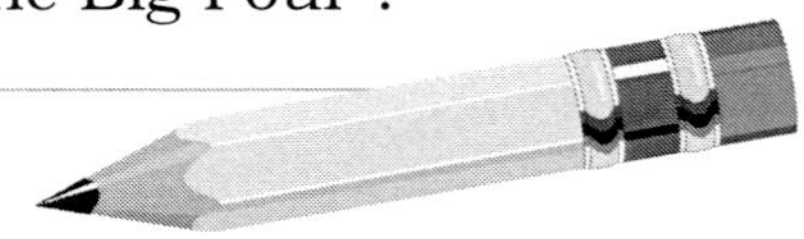

It's a Match!

Draw a line matching each member of The Big Four with the words that best describe the job he did.

Leland Stanford	**construction engineer** – plans and supervises construction projects
Charles Crocker	**fundraiser** – asks others for money and donations to help pay for a project
Mark Hopkins	**president** – makes sure the company has a plan and that everyone sticks to it
Collis P. Huntington	**accountant** – keeps track of how much money is spent and how it is spent

Leland Stanford—A Man with a Vision

Leland Stanford was one of "The Big Four." This was the group of men who imagined the Transcontinental Railroad and made it happen! Although all four men worked together, most people think Stanford was responsible for starting the project!

Stanford was from Sacramento, California. One day, he noticed a huge freight wagon being loaded for the treacherous trip over the Sierra Nevada mountains. Stanford knew that more and more people were coming west. He also knew that they needed a better and faster way of getting there. Stanford began talking about his ideas with other businessmen. They all agreed that the time had come for a railroad connection with the East!

Leland Stanford became the governor of California in 1863! Stanford University in California is named for this great visionary!

Do You Have What It Takes?

Leland Stanford accomplished what many said couldn't be done. Circle the attributes that are important in achieving success!

PATIENCE COMPLAINING

MISTAKES FAILURE

LAZINESS

ENCOURAGEMENT

PERSEVERANCE GIVING UP

TIME EXCUSES WHINING

OPTIMISM BRAINSTORMING

Two Railroads, One Track!

President Lincoln signed the Pacific Railroad Act in 1862. This law said two railroad companies would construct a railroad line that crossed the entire country. The Union Pacific would build west from Omaha, Nebraska, across the Great Plains. The Central Pacific would build east from Sacramento, California, through the Sierra Nevada mountain range.

The Central Pacific

Work on the Central Pacific began on January 8, 1863. The path it would follow had been planned by Theodore Judah many years before. Judah discovered a way to pass through the Sierras. It took him many years to convince the nation's leaders that his plan would work!

The Union Pacific

The other half of the plan was the Union Pacific Railroad. This railroad company was founded in Chicago, Illinois, on September 2, 1862. It took more than a year before workers began building the tracks! On December 2, 1863, the Union Pacific finally broke ground on the banks of the Missouri River. Both companies were now at work. Soon, the railroads would meet!

Tracking It!

Use a colored marker or pencil to trace the tracks laid by the Union Pacific. Use a different color to trace the tracks laid by the Central Pacific. Then answer the questions below.

1. Which railroad had more track to lay?

   ____

2. Which railroad do you think would have been more difficult to build?

   ____

   Why?______________________________

   ____

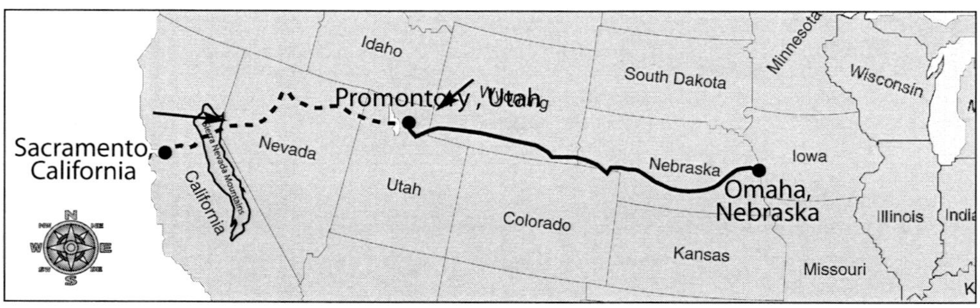

There Are Mountains in the Way!

Everyone knew that building a transcontinental railroad would be hard. Workers had to put together wooden bridges! Blast tunnels through mountains! Level out hundreds of miles of track bed! Lay the crossties and track! They also had to figure out how to move equipment, people, food, tools, metal, and wood to construction sites hundreds of miles away!

But no obstacle was bigger than the one that stood right in the middle of the tracks! It was the enormous mountain range called the Sierra Nevada. Getting through those mountains required thousands of workers. Those workers needed determination. They also needed the best tools and equipment available. Sadly, many of those workers died while building the railroad.

Central Pacific crews had the job of drilling 12 tunnels through the Sierra Nevada. Each tunnel was drilled by hand. Workers made it through just a few inches of rock a day!

Pointing the Way!

Railroad workers used compasses to help figure out which way the tracks should go. The arrow on a compass always points north. Once you know which way is north, you can figure out the other directions. Follow the instructions to create your own compass. Remember to hold it flat when you use it!

Materials: magnet, cork, large sewing needle, plastic cup filled with water

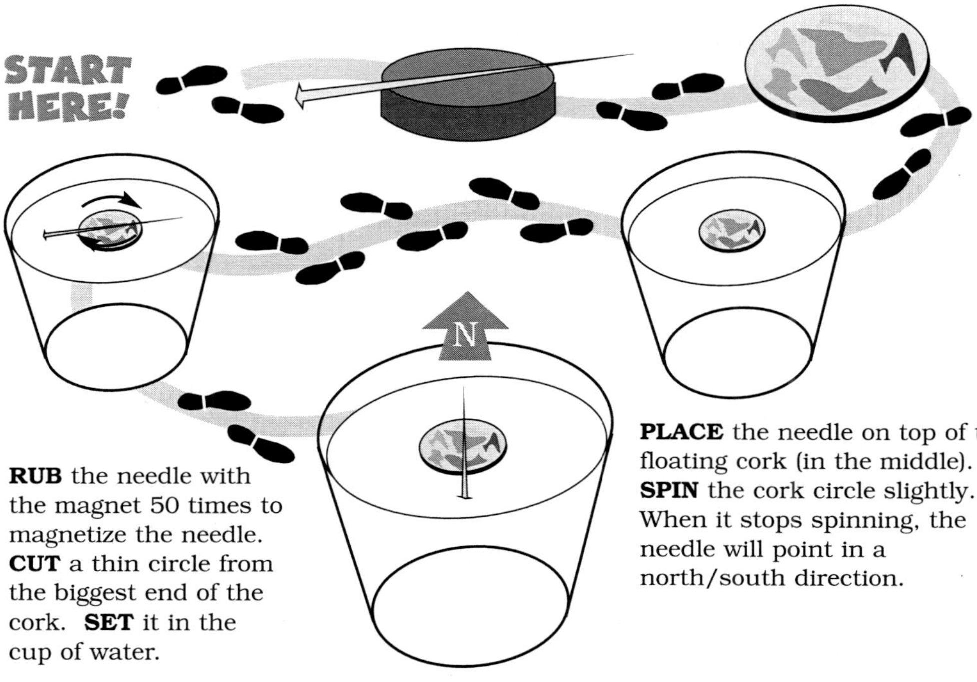

RUB the needle with the magnet 50 times to magnetize the needle. **CUT** a thin circle from the biggest end of the cork. **SET** it in the cup of water.

PLACE the needle on top of the floating cork (in the middle). **SPIN** the cork circle slightly. When it stops spinning, the needle will point in a north/south direction.

Who's Been Working on the Railroad?

Many of the workers on the Transcontinental Railroad were Irish or Chinese immigrants. Some were soldiers who had just finished fighting in the Civil War. At first, many people thought the Chinese were too small to do hard railroad work. But by the second year of work, most of the workers on the Central Pacific line were Chinese!

The Chinese workers could do what others could not—or what others wouldn't dare to try! Laying railroad tracks through the Sierras meant holes had to be blown through mountains! Chinese workers used techniques they had learned in China. They were lowered over the sides of cliffs in baskets they made themselves. While they dangled miles above the ground, they chipped away at the granite walls. Once a hole was big enough, they placed an explosive in it. Then, they scrambled back up the side of the mountain as quickly as they could!

Workers lived in railroad cars and made between $1 and $3 a day. They had to use that money to pay for food and a place to sleep. Irish workers made more than the Chinese workers. Plus, they didn't have to pay for a place to sleep. No fair!

Add It Up!

You are a Chinese railroad worker who makes $2 a day. Solve the math problems to find out how far your money will go!

1. You make $2 a day. How much do you make in a month with 30 days?

   $______________

2. The bed you sleep on costs $20 a month. Subtract this amount from the amount you make in a month with 30 days to find out how much you will have left.

   $______________

3. Now you must buy food for the month, which costs $10. Subtract this amount from amount you had after you paid for your bed to see what is left.

   $______________

4. You need to send half of the money you have left home to your family. How much is that?

   $______________

FAST FACT:
Bridge builders, blacksmiths, carpenters, engineers, masons, surveyors, teamsters, telegraphers, and cooks were also important jobs in helping to build the railroad.

Get That Railroad Out of Here!

Not everyone was excited about a railroad that traveled across the country. Explorers and settlers who came to the western territory changed the lives of people who had lived there for hundreds of years. Those people were the Plains Indians. The settlers spread disease. They also killed off the buffalo herds that Indians depended on for survival. They ruined the land. Native Americans called the railroad the "Iron Horse." The Iron Horse caused big problems between Native Americans and settlers. Eventually, the troubles turned into a war.

The Plains Indians did everything they could to stop the railroad. They shot at work crews. They raided station towns. They even made trains go off the track! In 1864, a group of Cavalrymen killed 150 Cheyenne and Arapaho Indians. Most of them were women and children. Those tribes got even by destroying the railroad town of Julesburg, Colorado.

Native American tribes soon realized they were no match for the technology and determination of the people who wanted to build the railroad. The Iron Horse continued on its way!

It's Poetry to Me!

An acrostic is a poem or series of lines in which certain letters, usually the first in each line, form a name, motto, or message. Use each letter in Iron Horse to tell something about the problems between the Plains Indians and white settlers. One example is given to get you started.

I -

R -

O -

N -

H - Herds of buffalo killed

O -

R -

S -

E -

Be Wary of the Weather!

Winter weather was one of the worst problems faced by workers along the Central Pacific line. Blizzards, avalanches, and freezing cold temperatures were very dangerous to workers.

The winter of 1866 was a terrible one in the Sierra Nevada! More than 40 storms blew through the mountains. Snow was 18 feet high in some places. Workers had to shovel around the clock. Imagine shoveling your driveway all day, every day, for several months! Crews built tunnels under the snow so they could get from their campsites to the work sites. They made wooden sheds over the train tracks to keep the snow off! The bad weather also made it difficult to get supplies and food to the workers.

Cold temperatures caused frostbite and pneumonia. Huge sheets of sliding snow, called avalanches, could strike at any time. Workers who got caught in an avalanche simply disappeared down the mountain!

Weather-Related!

Use the word bank to fill in the blanks below.

1. A cold weather injury that occurs when your skin gets so cold that it freezes
   ___ ___ ___ ___ ___ B ___ ___ ___
2. Severe weather that includes heavy snowfall and strong winds
   ___ ___ ___ ___ ___ A ___ ___
3. High piles of snow ___ ___ ___ ___ T ___
4. Built to keep snow off the railroad tracks ___ ___ ___ ___ S
5. Mountain range that had 44 storms in one winter!
   ___ ___ ___ R ___ ___   ___ ___ ___ ___ ___ ___
6. A sheet of quickly-moving snow and debris
   ___ ___ ___ ___ A ___ ___ ___ ___

Word Bank	
avalanche	blizzard
sheds	Sierra Nevada
frostbite	drifts

Travelin' Through

As quickly as the tracks were laid, towns sprung up along the railroad route. Railroad workers came to those towns. So did immigrants looking for a place to settle down. Some people came because they wanted to experience life in a railroad town. Most of these towns did not last long. People moved on as soon as a new stretch of track was finished.

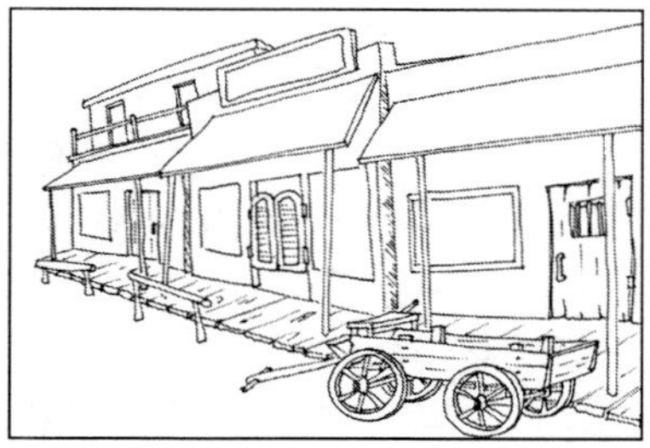

Men and women set up businesses. Because the new towns often emptied out just as quickly as they went up, the buildings were made of wood or canvas and could be taken apart and moved down the tracks.

Many things that were against the law happened in these railroad towns. They got the nickname of "Hell on Wheels." Most towns didn't have sheriffs or policemen. Crime became a problem. Sometimes, citizens of a town had to take matters into their own hands! In Laramie, Wyoming, in 1868, crime was everywhere. Finally, an angry group of shopkeepers and railroad workers battled a gang of outlaws in the streets. They chased the scoundrels out of town!

Think About It!

Write your answers to the questions below. Be sure to use complete sentences!

1. Why do we have laws?

____

____

2. Is it important to follow laws?__________________

   Why or why not?_______________________________

____

3. What happens when people don't follow laws?

____

____

4. Who is in charge of enforcing laws?

____

____

New Industries, New Ideas

The Transcontinental Railroad changed the United States! It let people travel more quickly. It let businesses ship their goods more easily. It helped many industries grow. Mining, farming, and cattle-raising businesses started along the railroad.

The railroad changed something else. It allowed Americans to feel that they were part of one big country. Before, the United States was a country divided in half. Now, as people traveled, they could look out the train windows. They could see the forests, prairies, mountains, and rivers that made up their country! They could also see the towns and cities where their fellow Americans lived.

Picture This!

You are a passenger traveling from Nebraska to California on the new Transcontinental Railroad. As you look out the window, you are amazed by the beauty of the United States. Write a postcard to your family in Nebraska telling them about what you've seen.

The Golden Spike

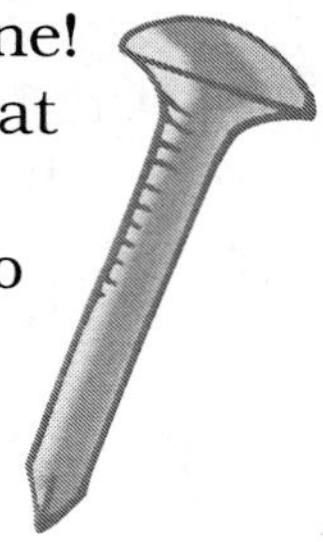

It took six years of back-breaking work. Finally, the railroad was done! Representatives of the Central Pacific and the Union Pacific railroads met at Promontory, Utah, on May10, 1869. They held a ceremony to celebrate a dream come true! Leland Stanford drove a golden spike into the ground to represent the joining of the railroads and the country. As soon as the ceremony ended, a telegraph message was sent to both the East Coast and West Coast. The message was one word: "DONE."

The whole country celebrated!

FAST FACT: The golden spike driven into the ground in Promontory, Utah, has an inscription on it that reads: *May God continue the unity of our Country as this Railroad unites the two great Oceans of the world.*

Spread the News!

Pretend you live in Utah where the railroads met. Write a letter to your best friend sharing the news of the Transcontinental Railroad and what it means to the country.

Fame & Fortune

Completing the Transcontinental Railroad made Leland Stanford, Collis P. Huntington, Charles Crocker, and Mark Hopkins famous—and rich! Help The Big Four tell their amazing success story by designing the front page of the newspaper below.

Spread the News!

Help the travelers celebrate the joining of the Transcontinental Railroad by designing the front page of your own newspaper! Write an article about the journey on the rails.

1. Masthead (Name of newspaper-make one up!)
2. Date Happened (Write on this line.)
3. Dateline (Place where happened)
4. BIG HEADLINE!
5. Tell the news!
6. Photo (Draw a picture of a train in the box.)
7. Sidebar (Put a quotation or trivia fact in lower right box.)
8. Editor (Hey, that's you!)

The Future of Railroads

Building a railroad through a mountain range was an amazing accomplishment. Many people thought it couldn't be done! Today, there are railroads that run under water! The Bay Area Rapid Transit System in California travels under the San Francisco Bay! Japan has a high speed train powered by magnetic force! France has a high-speed train powered by electricity! Because trains are so fuel efficient, some people think they are the transportation of the future.

Imagine it!

Draw a picture of what you think trains will look like in the year 2050. Will they travel under water—or through space?

Railroad Safety Rules

Building railroad tracks today isn't nearly as dangerous as it once was. But every year in the United States people are injured or die on railroad tracks. That's because they forget some basic train safety rules!

Rule #1—The train always wins. Trains can weigh as much as 10,000 tons. It can take nearly one mile for a train to stop. It is impossible for a person or a car to outrace a train.

Rule #2—NEVER play on or near railroad tracks. It's just too dangerous!

Rule #3—Obey railroad signs and signals. A flashing light means a train is coming and no one should be near the track.

Rule #4—Always stand at least 10 feet back from a moving train. Rocks and debris thrown by the train can injure anyone standing too close.

Rule #5—Only cross railroad tracks at places that say it is OK to do so. If you try to cross anywhere else, you could be in big trouble with the police!

X Marks the Spot!

Use the code below to learn the name of the x-shaped sign at a railroad crossing.

____ ____ ____ ____ ____ ____ ____ ____ ____

FAST FACT! Be careful—trains often look like they are moving slower than they really are!

Transcontinental Railroad Trivia

Let's see what you've learned! Read the Transcontinental Trivia below and circle True or False.

TRUE/FALSE 1. It took more than half a year to travel the Oregon Trail.

TRUE/FALSE 2. The discovery of gold in California was an important reason for building the railroad.

TRUE/FALSE 3. The men responsible for imagining and completing the railroad were called The Super Six.

TRUE/FALSE 4. Native Americans welcomed the Transcontinental Railroad.

TRUE/FALSE 5. Weather was one of the biggest obstacles to building the railroad.

TRUE/FALSE 6. Theodore Roosevelt was the American president who signed the papers giving permission to build the Transcontinental Railroad.

TRUE/FALSE 7. Immigrants played an important role in building the railroad.

TRUE/FALSE 8. The towns built along the railroad were safe places to live.

TRUE/FALSE 9. Laying tracks through mountains was a difficult and dangerous job.

TRUE/FALSE 10. Trains are rarely used today.

TRUE/FALSE 11. You should never play on or near railroad tracks.

TRUE/FALSE 12. A flashing light on a railroad track means that a train is coming.

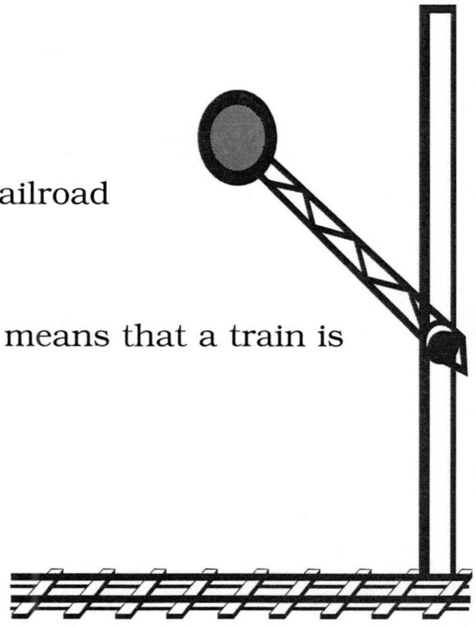

Additional Resources

BOOKS

Railroad Fever: Building the Transcontinental Railroad 1830-1870 by Monica Halpern

Ten Mile Day by Mary Ann Fraser

The Journal of Sean Sullivan: A Transcontinental Railroad Worker: Nebraska and Points West, 1867 by William Durbin

WEBSITES

Transcontinental Railroad American Experience
www.pbs.org/wgbh/amex/tcrr/

Central Pacific Railroad Photographic History Museum
cprr.org/Museum/Chinese.html

The Virtual Museum of the City of San Francisco, Driving the Last Spike
http://www.sfmuseum.org/hist1/rail.html

MUSEUMS

The Union Pacific Railroad Museum, Council Bluffs, Iowa
The Central Pacific Railroad Museum: http://cprr.org
California State Railroad Museum, Sacramento, California
Golden Spike National Historic Site, Promontory Summit, Utah

Glossary

immigrant: a person who leaves one country to live permanently in another country

Native American: any member of the peoples living in North or South America before the Europeans arrived

obstacle: something that stands in the way of progress or achievement

outlaw: a person who is rebellious or does not obey the law

pioneer: a colonist, explorer, or settler of a new land or region

prospector: someone who explores an area for mineral deposits, such as gold or silver

spike: a long metal nail

telegraph: a message sent using short, rapid electric impulses transmitted either by wire or radio to a receiving station

transcontinental: extending across a continent

visionary: a person who finds creative solutions to problems

Answer Key

Page 10: 4, 6, 1, 3, 2, 5

Page 12: Stanford, president; Crocker, construction engineer; Hopkins, accountant; Huntington, fundraiser

Page 13: patience, mistakes, encouragement, perseverance, time, optimism, brainstorming

Page 14: 1. The Union Pacific had more track to lay; 2. The Central Pacific would have been more difficult to build because it had to cross mountains.

Page 16: 1. $60; 2. $40; 3. $30; 4. $15

Page 18: 1. frostbite; 2. blizzard; 3. drifts; 4. sheds; 5. Sierra Nevada; 6. avalanche

Page 25: 1. True; 2. True; 3. False; 4. False; 5. True; 6. False; 7. True; 8. False; 9. True; 10. False; 11. True; 12. True

Index